Alex Is My Friend

MARISABINA RUSSO

Greenwillow Books New York

For Mabel, Lou,
Elyse, Melinda,
Justin, and,
of course, Alex

GOUACHE PAINTS WERE USED
FOR THE FULL-COLOR ART.
THE TEXT TYPE IS
ITC MODERN NO. 216 MEDIUM.

PRINTED IN HONG KONG BY SOUTH CHINA
PRINTING COMPANY (1988) LTD.

FIRST EDITION   10 9 8 7 6 5 4 3 2 1

LIBRARY OF CONGRESS
CATALOGING-IN-PUBLICATION DATA

RUSSO, MARISABINA.
ALEX IS MY FRIEND/BY MARISABINA RUSSO.
     P.   CM.
SUMMARY: EVEN THOUGH ALEX IS A DWARF AND
SOMETIMES HAS TO USE A WHEELCHAIR BECAUSE
OF THE OPERATION HE HAD ON HIS BACK,
HIS FRIEND DOES NOT MIND BECAUSE THEY
STILL HAVE GOOD TIMES TOGETHER.
ISBN 0-688-10418-5 (TRADE).
ISBN 0-688-10419-3 (LIB.)
[1. DWARFS—FICTION.
2. PHYSICALLY HANDICAPPED—FICTION.
3. FRIENDSHIP—FICTION.]
I. TITLE.   PZ7.R9192A1 1992
[E]—DC20 90-24643 CIP AC

Alex is my friend. We met a
long time ago when we
were little. This is how we met.

We were both at a soccer game.
Our big sisters played on the same
team. I was sleeping in my stroller,
and Alex was running around me
making noises like a truck. Mama
asked Alex to play somewhere else,
because she didn't want me to
wake up.

But I woke up, anyway. There
was Alex's face real close to
mine. He said, "Hi!" I closed my
eyes again.

We started seeing each other every Sunday at our sisters' soccer games. We grew older, and Alex and I became friends. We would chase each other or kick balls or tell silly stories. Alex always had a funny joke.

We shared our snacks, like pretzels and apples and juice. We shared our toys, like crayons and super-heroes and cars. Sometimes we traded our hats. Sometimes we even watched our sisters play soccer.

We always go to each other's birth-day parties. I don't know why, but Alex invites girls to his parties. He likes girls, especially Amy. He told me he's going to marry her. I think that's a dumb idea.

One birthday, when Alex was turning six and I was still five, I noticed something funny about Alex. He was smaller than I was. I asked Mama, "If Alex is older than I am, why isn't he bigger than I am?"

Mama said, "Alex is always going to be small. It is how he was born. He is still getting older, just like you, still going to school learning new things, still thinking like a big boy, but his body will grow very slowly."

"You mean even when he's a teen-ager, he'll be small?" I asked.

"Yes," said Mama.

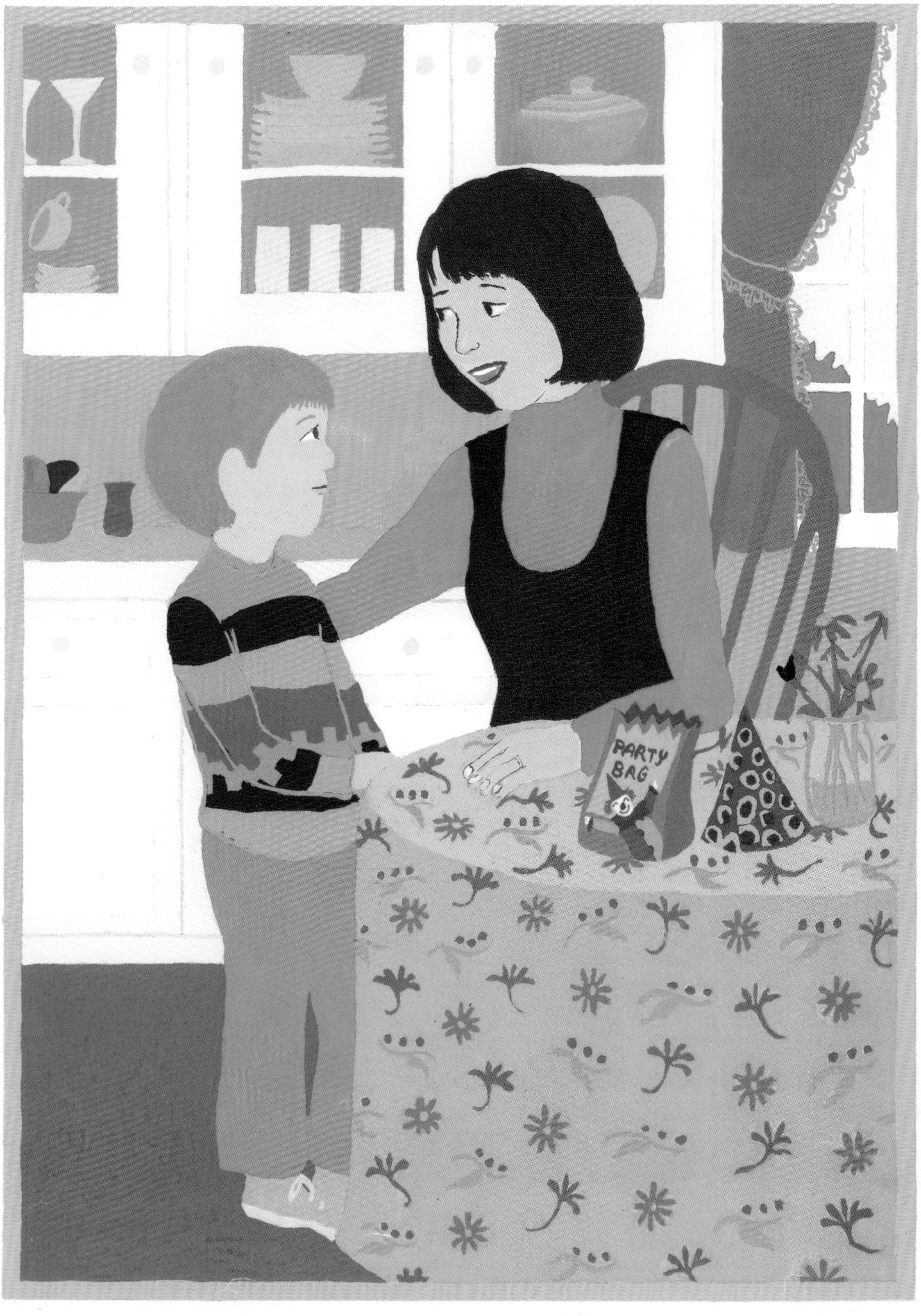
PARTY
BAG

It didn't matter to me that Alex was small, but then he started having trouble with his back, and he couldn't really run anymore. One day Mama told me, "Alex has to go to a hospital for an operation on his back."

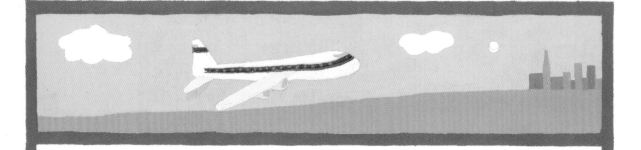

Alex and his mother had to
take an airplane to another city
in another state to get to the
hospital. They were gone for
a week.

After they came home, Mama said,
"Let's go buy Alex a present and visit
him."
We went to the toy store. I wanted to
get him a remote control car or a kite,
but Mama said no.
"It has to be something he can play
with in bed. He has to stay in bed for
a few months so his back can heal."
We got Alex a book and a hand puppet.

I was so excited the day we were
going to visit Alex. When his
mother opened the door, I rushed
in yelling, "Hi, Alex!"
Then I saw him lying on this bed
in the middle of the living room.
He had a weird metal ring around
his head. It looked scary.

"Hey, Ben!" said Alex in a loud voice.
"Look at all this candy I've got."
   It sounded just like Alex, even though
he looked like an alien. Mama handed
me the present to give to Alex.
"Ben, did you ever hear this joke?" said
   Alex. "How can you tell an elephant's
   been in your refrigerator?"
   I shrugged.
"By the footprints in the butter!" said
   Alex, and we both started laughing.
   I gave Alex my present, and he gave
   me a lollipop.

For a long time Alex didn't come to soccer games. I really missed him. Then he started coming in a wheelchair. After a while he could walk again, but he couldn't run. So we sat on a blanket and played games. Now he can walk and run, and he only needs his wheelchair in school to get down the halls faster. He told me he hates his wheelchair.

Our sisters are still on the same
soccer team, so every Sunday Alex
and I get to see each other. Now I'm
a lot bigger than Alex, but he's still
older. I can run faster than Alex,
but he still tells funnier jokes. We
don't chase each other anymore,
because I always win.

We play games on the blanket
or tell stories or color pictures of
dinosaurs. Alex is little and I'm
big, but it doesn't really matter.
It doesn't really matter, because
Alex is my friend.